James Krüss "Der wohltemperierte Leierkasten"
Text © 1989 CBJ Verlag an imprint of Random House Munich
Illustrations © NordSüd Verlag AG
First published in Switzerland under the title *Weil bald Ostern ist*
English translation copyright © 2012 by North-South Books Inc., New York 10017.

Adapted from James Krüss's poem "Osterbotschaft"
First published in the United States, Great Britain, Canada, Australia, and New Zealand in 2012
by North-South Books, Inc., an imprint of NordSüd Verlag AG, CH-8005 Zürich, Switzerland.

Translated by David Henry Wilson.
Designed by Christy Hale.
Distributed in the United States by North-South Books Inc., New York 10017.
Library of Congress Cataloging-in-Publication Data is available.
ISBN: 978-0-7358-4070-6 (trade edition)
1 3 5 7 9 ● 10 8 6 4 2
Printed in Germany by Grafisches Centrum Cuno GmbH & Co. KG, 39240 Calbe, November 2011.
www.northsouth.com

Wake Up, It's Easter!

Adapted from a poem by James Krüss

Illustrated by Frauke Weldin

NorthSouth

New York / London

Mr. Croak the raven
Is sitting in the sun
Preparing Easter messages
To take to everyone.

He puts his traveling clothes on,
Then as fast as he can fly,
He goes to visit Vicki Vole
Down amid the rye.

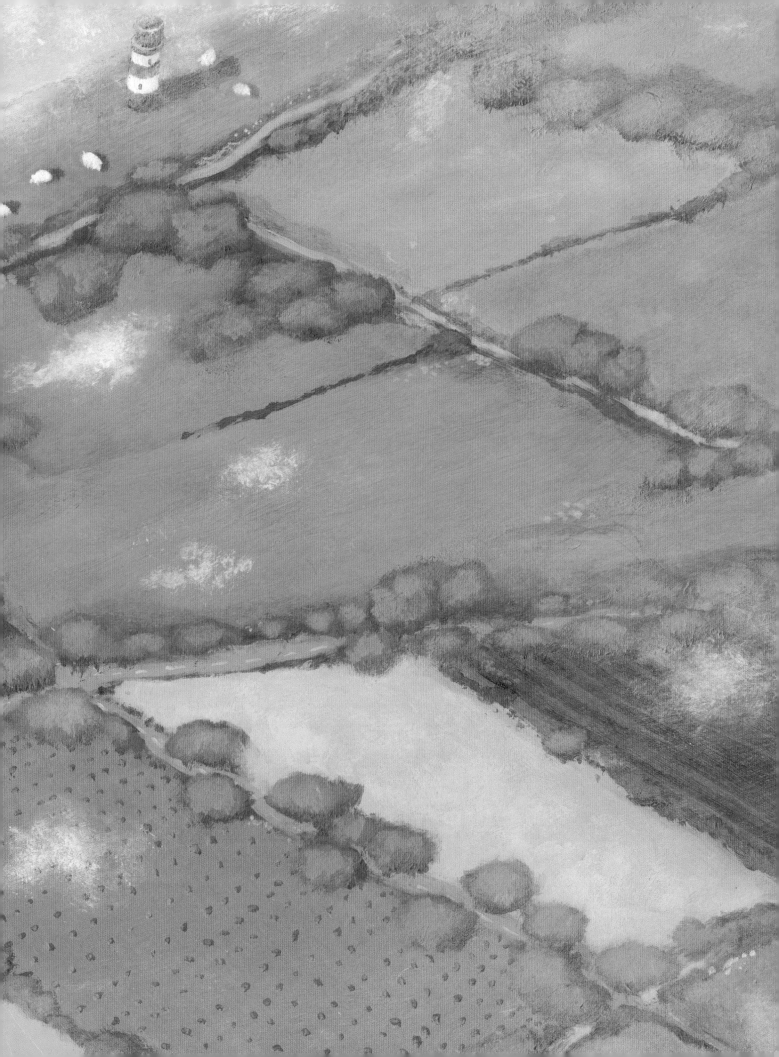

To see him little Vicki
Is really not too glad.
She's learned from past experience
That ravens can be bad.

But Mr. Croak speaks softly,
And his tone is most polite:
"Excuse me, Easter's coming soon.
The sun is shining bright."

"Well, so it is," squeaks Vicki,
"And the sky's a royal blue."
She freshens up for Eastertime,
As all good creatures do.

Down tunnels lit by glowworms
As bright as any moon
She runs to tell Rob Rabbit
That Easter's coming soon.

She wakes him with a tickle—
Itchy-kitchy-koo!
With twitching nose, wide-eyed he asks:
"What can I do for you?"

Vicki Vole is quite surprised.
"Come on, you silly loon;
The sun is bright, the sky is blue,
And Easter's coming soon."

"Eh, what? You say it's Easter?
I'm off!" he cries out loud.
And—*whoosh!*—he leaves poor Vicki covered
In a dusty cloud.

Rob bounds across the meadows
With a smile upon his face,
Turns somersaults because the world
Is such a lovely place.

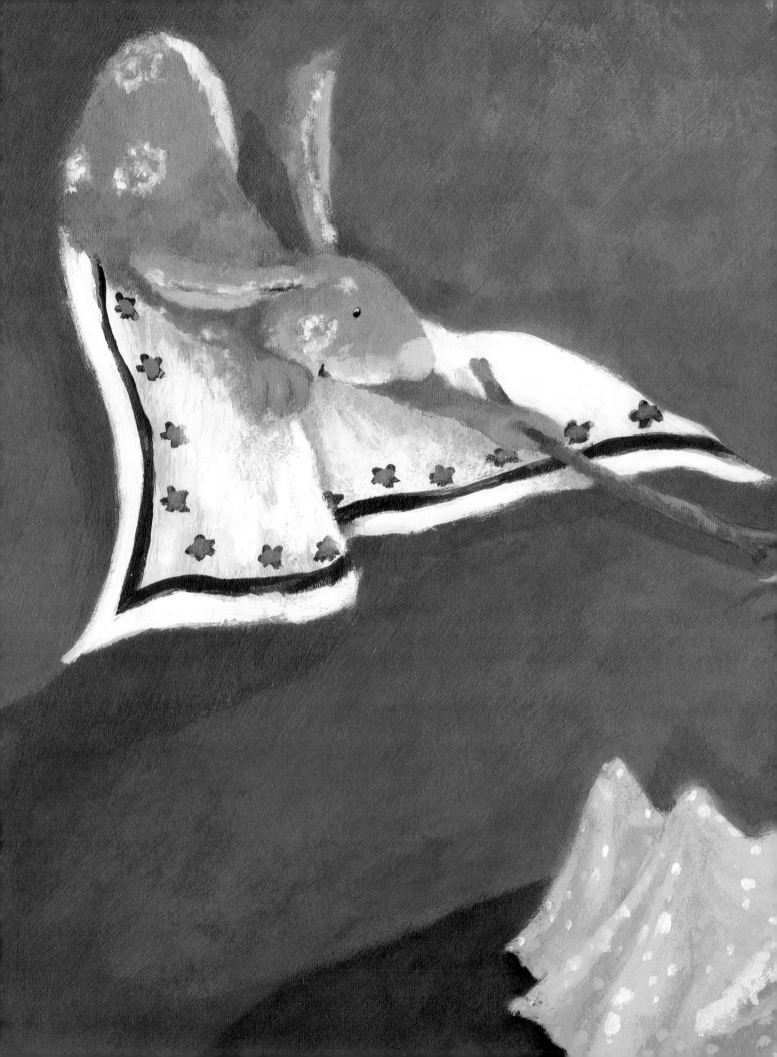

He goes to all the rabbits.
"Wake up! It's nearly noon!
Come on, the sun is shining bright,
And Easter's coming soon!"

And so the happy rabbits
Go romping far and near,
And suddenly the whole wide world
Knows Eastertime is here.